I0451821

KEEP YOUR UGLY TO YOURSELF, & Don't Give Your Pretty Away

by Nia Zola

from: *Africa Untold Tales*

ISBN: 978-1-967860-09-8

Paperback Version

Table of Contents

Keep Your Ugly to Yourself & Don't Give Your Pretty Away

Mosi and Adama

Once upon a time, in the vibrant and bustling African kingdom of Uzuri, two men lived in stark contrast. One was Mosi, a young, humble farmer whose heart was as vast and golden as the fields he tilled. Yet, his appearance was considered unfortunate by many: his nose was large and crooked, his ears stuck out like the sails of a sailboat, and his gait was awkward. Mosi didn't know why, but it was because one of his legs was crooked, so it was shorter than the other. Despite this, he greeted everyone with kindness, offering his help without expecting anything in return.

The other was Adama, the 25-year-old son of the wealthiest merchant in Uzuri. Adama's beauty was legendary; women in the kingdom sang songs about his chiseled jawline, gleaming smile, and eyes that sparkled like stars. But behind his handsome face lay a dark and selfish soul.

Adama thrived on deception and cruelty, taking what he wanted without regard for others.

The Curse of the Half Curse

One fateful day, the village oracle, dressed in all red and many ornate beads, stood on a platform in the market square. She was surrounded by many attentive men and women of the kingdom. Madam Zubedi, announced, "Last night, while we all slept, a curse was sowed into our kingdom. Some of you may have already noticed that one half of your field is normal and green, and the other half is brown and withered. Overnight. This is the curse of the half curse, where the enemy messes you up half the way so you just think it's a coincidence or that you did something wrong, when really it is a curse.

The people acknowledged and were vocal and loud about this problem. How would they make a living? How would they feed their families? They wouldn't have anything to bring to market.

"Yeah," cried out an older farmer, "Everything was fine in my fields last night, I checked. It was fine, but now—".

"Who did this?" blurted out another man.

"It was the curse of a spiritual enemy of this kingdom," answered Zubedi.

"Where are they? Let me at them!" yelled another from the crowd. Many screamed and it seemed that a mob was forming.

There's no one to get at; this is a spiritual enemy, you can't see them, there is no person to fight. This has to be solved spiritually, else a spiritual drought that even rain can't fix would happen to our land and it could devastate Uzuri.

Because it is a spiritual battle, it can only be fought in a certain way. Only the purest heart," she continued. "can uncover the ancient well hidden in the forest. We only need one gourd of water from that well and it will keep us from being wiped out by the enemy that sows spiritual curses while we sleep. It is the key to saving our kingdom."

Who will go to the sacred forest?

Men stepped up, yelling, "I'll go, I'll go---"

Only the Purest Heart

Madam Zubedi warned, "Only the purest heart can get what we need from the sacred well to save this land."

Pure heart? the men began to mumble as they stepped back. They knew their hearts weren't pure. Their thoughts weren't pure, their actions weren't pure. They hoped no one knew they weren't pure souls, but they, themselves knew. So, they began to step back and became quiet.

Soon there was no one standing in front of Madam Zubedi volunteering for the journey.

Which one will it be? Who will go? Any candidates? Any suggestions? Any nominations?

There was a brief pause and then, the people, mostly the women cheered for Adama. They liked chanting his name anyway.

Adama stepped up like a hero and proclaimed that he was the best one for the journey, there was nobody taller, smarter, wiser, more buff than him. He would be perfect for this adventure. When Madam Zubedi said there was an ancient well, Adama heard there is ancient wealth and he was all about going to get wealth. This is why he stepped up.

Now, was Adama's heart pure?

To Adama, he thinks that life is an act and you can act your way through it. He planned to *act* pure hearted – when he got to the ancient wealth.

Madam Zubedi was skeptical that Adama could do it, so she offered, "Anyone else? He was confused and insulted, "I'm definitely going."

Mosi stepped up and said, stammering, "I, I, I'm taller. I'll go. Then he stated his motive for volunteering: "If this is a dire situation, then I want to also go to help the kingdom, as well as save my own home and farm."

Almost no one cheered for Mosi, a single slow clap was all that could be heard. Well, at least someone believed in him.

The king of Uzuri quickly got involved, more desperate to save the land than anything else. He consulted the Elders of the land and along with Madam Zubedi they concluded that only the purest heart could even reach the Sacred Forest.

"Only the purest heart would find the well once they got there," she said.

"And only the purest heart would be able to retrieve the sacred water," chimed in one of the Elders.

"And," added, the last Elder, "Only the purest heart will be able to return to us."

"This is a dangerous mission," said the king." They mused out loud to one another.

Selfishly, the Elders and Madam Zubedi and the king decided that they would not tell either of these two who wanted to go on the mission, but they had the nerve to hope for themselves that one of them, at least one of them, would return.

"What are the chances that they both reach the well and get the enchanted water and come back to this kingdom of Uzuri?" asked the King.

"We don't know, it's never happened before," said Madam Zubedi.

Princess Neema

Princess Neema, the beautiful daughter of the king, was sweet-natured, and very feminine. She was the kind of feminine that a girl or a young lady becomes when she is allowed to be a girl. When she doesn't have to do the duties that men should do. When she doesn't have to take on the roles that a man should be taking on and completing, she is allowed to be 100 percent female. Princess Neema was always in a beautiful dress, her flowing hair was natural but brushed prettily with a tiara adorning it.

She listened attentively, loved people, understood others' point of view and smiled easily, even as she offered solutions for those who approached her. After all she was a princess and did have royal duties as well as royal authority under her father.

Normally in a very good mood, Princess Neema overheard the conversation between Madame Zubedi, her own father, and the three Elders of the kingdom. After the guests had all left, later that afternoon, a fired-up princess approached her father saying, Dad, you can't let anyone go out there into all that danger. Dad!

The king said, "We must, or all of us will perish."

"Dad! Have a heart!" she screamed storming off.

One Rugged Man

Adama, believing that he should be the one chosen, secretly was eager for glory and riches, immediately announced his quest. He started competing against Mosi, who was not competing with him. Adama ran his why he should win campaign by boasting to the villagers, "I, the most capable and the most handsome man in Uzuri, will find this ancient wealth and save you all!" He said this all day, every day to whomever would listen, as if the people were voting on which of them should go.

Adama lost sight of the fact that only one with the purest heart could even get into the Sacred Forest to get what the kingdom needed, and return back to Uzuri. He somehow didn't understand that you can't vote on who has a pure heart. Even though people can see and feel the pureness of a man's heart, voting on it because they like you, or you're handsome or rich, does not make your heart pure. And, especially to be deemed to have a pure heart is not because of popularity or a rich father.

The same man who used to dress in the finest finery, suits imported from Europe, and steal apples from market vendors was now pretending to be humble. Daily, leading up to the king's decision of who should go to the Sacred Forest, Adama could be found walking about the village dressed as a rugged man ready to go on a quest to save the kingdom. Many cheered him on, dazzled by his charm, and thinking that he had changed, never realizing he said, wealth and was going to look for wealth, and not a well, he was going to the Sacred Forest to look for ancient wealth, not to look for the ancient well that had the water that could save the land and farms of Uzuri.

Mosi, though ridiculed by the villagers, because he didn't look muscular, was motivated not by fame or money but by his genuine concern for his people. "If I can help save anyone, this land, the kingdom, my farm, or my home," he thought, "then it is worth the risk."

Those are the words of a man with a pure heart. It can be voted upon if you know such a man and if you know that man to be goodhearted, kind, or considerate. But in a contest for the tallest man, if the people vote for the most popular man, that will not make the man tall. Height is inherent in the man. A man is born with a pure heart and nurtures it throughout his life to keep it pure or make it even purer.

An unloved person will be like an abandoned or unnurtured heart will lose purity and eventually it will show.

By a man's ways, you shall know him.

Half & Half

The kingdom was divided. Exactly half wanted Adama to go to the ancient well and save them because he looked rich and capable. And the other half wanted Mosi because they thought he had a pure heart. But the choice was not up to the people; this was not a popularity contest.

The king made a proclamation that **both** Adama and Mosi would go on this mission. As they both stood before him in the palace, the king, half wondering and half hoping that more men would have been standing up volunteering to go, said, "You two can work together."

Adama wasn't having that and so he said, "Your Majesty, with all due respect, I would like to go on this mission alone.

"Oh?" questioned the king, with an eyebrow raised.

"Your majesty, I'd like to take the mission alone," Adama repeated.

Wondering why, the king spoke again saying, "Very well." Knowing that those were the only two who volunteered to go, the King continued, "Very well, you both can go. And, may the best man win," he said half-heartedly. Not really expecting that either of them would win or even come back to the kingdom. The king tried very hard to hide the look of doom that had crawled on his face.

He was king and it was up to him to solve kingdom problems, but every day the curse of the half curse was spreading to fields throughout the kingdom. The curse caused one half of every farmer's crop to turn brown while the other half was healthy and strong.

Now you see why they had to find someone with a pure heart, because none of the people in positions of power had any purity, they were all selfish. Very selfish. And Madam Zubedi, well she was dressed like a red cobra anyway, so what do we expect of her?

The king was desperate to save his people--, well, to save himself and his position as king--, so he declared that whoever found the well would receive great wealth and the hand of his beautiful daughter, Princess Neema, in marriage.

The two "winners" of the who-would-go portion of this contest, that Adama had created in his own head, were still standing before the king as he made this statement and brought out Princess Neema to stand near all the gold that would go to the winner.

When Adama saw the gold, his eyes lit up, he never really saw Princess Neema and really stopped listening when the king said the words wealth, or gold, or whatever he said.

Wow, thought Adama, I'm going to look for ancient wealth and when I get back, there's more wealth. Oh yeah, he muttered to himself, smiling. Oh yeah.

When Mosi saw Princess Neema, his eyes lit up. He had seen the Princess in the village from time to time, not only was she beautiful, but she was also gracious and kindhearted to people.

Once she paid for the food of a person who didn't have enough money at the market. What a lovely person he thought to himself. He didn't even hear the king say anything about gold or wealth; Princess Neema was so amazing. Gold, not really. *King who?* It was Princess Neema that had Mosi's attention.

Not only for the people and his own farmland, but to marry such a wonderful woman would be a dream come true. Mosi wanted to win and was determined to do so.

Each thought the prize was awesome and they each wanted to win.

What a man sees as valuable, he will see as a prize, and he will cherish it.

The Journey Starts

The day of the Journey arrived. The two men stood in the market square surrounded by many of the kingdom who came to see them off and cheer them on. Adama was dressed in his rugged man gear that he had created for himself, as if he was a Hollywood hero who had already gone to wardrobe. Where did he even get the stuff he wore, many people wondered.

Mosi, had on one of his usual outfits, an African tunic to endure the heat of the sun and pants. He looked pretty much the same as he looked every day. In his bag he had short pants, just in case it got really hot. And a throw, for when it got chilly at night. He didn't really know the weather.

Mosi also had a gourd he had tied with a rope over one shoulder, for the water that he would collect from the **ancient well** that is in the Sacred Forest.

Adama had no collection vessel for water. Remember, though, Adama doesn't even know that he's going to fetch water to save the kingdom from the curse of the Half Curse. No, he thinks he's going to get ancient wealth.

These are two men of opposites; they even set out in opposite directions at the start of the journey.

Adama, convinced of his superiority, ignored the advice of the elders and took shortcuts through treacherous lands. Along the way, he encountered travelers in need but turned them away, sneering, "I have no time for weaklings."

An Eye for the Ladies

Adama met two beautiful women in a village along the way but close to the Sacred Forest. He liked both of them. Lamina and Kwamboka were best friends, but that didn't stop Adama. He decided to chat them both up.

He convinced one to let him come to her house and stay a while and she did because he told her that he was looking to be married. He took what he wanted from her and then as he was leaving he cruelly said, "You weren't the prettiest one anyway, I liked your friend, Kwamboka better. Plus, you're not rich enough for me." Adama was lying; he loved this girl from first sight, but the evil in his heart would make him do and say the worst things to people, even to women.

Lamina hung her head and began to weep because she had given away her virtues to this, this – whatever he is.

He then went to the other woman's house. The evil in him drew him there where he took her virtues against her will telling her that he couldn't help himself, something just came over him. When he was done with her, he left telling her that she wasn't beautiful enough for him. I mean, he said, just look at me, how could I possibly stay with you or marry *you*?

The curse of the Half Curse that blighted half the land in Uzuri had also turned half of Adama's heart dry, brown and unalive. However, that was the side of his heart that he had chosen to listen to. Seems the curse wasn't just affecting the land and farms of Uzuri, but now it was touching the heart of the people there? Could this really be happening?

By this time, the first girl, Lamina pulled herself together again. She came out of her house and met her friend Kwamboka who was also very upset because she had fallen for the same lines from Adama.

They consoled one another. Each of the friends compared notes on this Adama, and quickly came to their senses. They asked one another, What did we see in that ugly man anyway?

Lamina, it's like we were so desperate to get a husband that we thought that by giving ourselves away we could win that man's heart. Lamina sobbed even louder because she secretly loved Adama so much.

"Lamina, don't cry," said Kwamboka, trying to comfort her, "You're so much prettier when you are not crying. Let's not let mistakenly sleeping with Adama take our pretty away.

"You're right Kwamboka, we cannot let him take our beauty away. We are still young women, and we can get husbands. Look at all the men in this village who are attracted to us."

"Yeah, but we never gave into them, we kept our virginity. We kept our virtues and our self-worth."

Kwamboka suggested, "We should report him—"

"No!" exclaimed Lamina, "that will ruin our reputations."

"Oh, I guess you're right," replied Kwamboka.

They cried for another moment and then decided they would fight back. Full of rage, they went back into their houses and got whatever they could use as weapons, or found rocks on the ground, anything they could find and then chased him. Adama was still standing around the village trying to talk to yet another woman. Is he serious, right now, the women thought. They yelled to him and started to chase him, but he didn't even run fast, he thought this was fun--, mocking the women.

Some other women joined the two offended women and gave chase with them.

This village was united, if one was hurt, they all were hurt.

But then the men in the town saw the chase, they joined in a mob to beat him up. He started to run faster then, these men were Kenyans, they could run! Adama luckily got away from them, and didn't lose his life--, that day.

They told him if he ever, ever, ever set foot in this town again or even if they saw him anywhere, they would make him unalive, forever.

It only took days or weeks for these men, even though they were defensive of Lamina and Kwamboka, to realize that these two had given away their virtue, their virginity, and from that day the men of the village who had been interested in them were no longer interested.

These two ladies begin to look ugly in the sight of the single men of the village. **Ladies:** *Do not give your pretty away. The ugly of another can transfer to you, if you get too close to them. Even if you agree or* *if they steal it, your pretty could be up for grabs by those with a selfish or an evil heart.*

Adama, with his ugly ways, had struck again. This was far worse than stealing apples from the market vendors. He had destroyed their lives, he had destroyed their opportunities for marriage, at least in their village among the men who knew they were no longer virgins. Adama, believing himself special, better, and more important than anyone, laughed as he ran away. This was a new level of evil, even for Adama, who always had a malicious side.

The Other Path

Mosi, on the other hand, followed the path with patience and humility. He helped an old woman carry firewood, rescued a bird tangled in a net, and shared his meager food with a little child. The old woman cooked him a good meal because Mosi had helped her. Mosi told her where he was going and she said that it was good that he ate because it is never wise to go to the Sacred Forest hungry, there are too many temptations there, and there are many beautiful things there that no one should eat.

She told Mosi to stop by there on his way home from the Forest and she would make another good meal for him to keep him strong for his journey home.

The little girl's mom was thankful that he shared his meal with her little daughter so she gave Mosi some water in a container that he could drink along the way, so he would not get parched. She told him, it is not good to go to the sacred forest thirsty because all the water there is not good for drinking. Then she said as he was leaving, when you get to the forest, speak to it; it's alive. Say your name, where you are from and what your business is there.

Oh, and after you leave there, stop by here again and we will have more fresh water for you for your journey back to your village.

Each act of kindness earned him blessings from the grateful recipients. The bright and beautiful bird he had saved flew from tree to tree to lead the way and soon he had reached the Sacred Forest.

Stumbling Blocks

Espionage and sabotage were not past Adama because he was determined to reach the Sacred Forest first. After all, he wanted to find the ancient wealth and he wanted it to all be his. He was strong and planned to carry as much of it back as he could, then he would return with an expedition to gather up the rest.

Adama was used to nice things, after all, his father was the richest merchant in the kingdom of Uzuri, but Adama felt it was time he earned his own wealth and showed his father how this was really done.

A man who competes with his own father shows a lot about what is in his heart.

By crooked means, Adama had already discovered the most commonly used path to the Sacred Forest, and he also knew the villages and the stops along the way. He knew the heart of Mosi, who was soft hearted and tenderhearted, a bleeding heart, almost. If someone was in trouble, he would stop to help them. Adama was counting on this, as it would slow Mosi down so Adama could get to the Sacred Forest first. He was determined to win.

In a village on the way to the Forest, there was an old widow woman who would go to gather firewood daily in the same place. There was a firewood seller close to her home. Adama went to that firewood vendor and bought all the firewood that he had for that day, so he ran out. Adama even paid the firewood seller extra money to take all that he had. Adama told the wood seller that he would send two men by to pick it up later and not to sell it to anyone else. That was a lie and he knew that no one would come back and pick up that firewood.

He knew that the old woman would have to walk an extra mile or two to buy wood from another man and then trek back to her home with it. He estimated when Mosi would be coming through, and his calculations were right. Mosi stopped to help the old woman.

There was an old man on the original path that Adama took. Adama paid two other men to carry the old man to another spot where he would beg, and that spot happened to be on the path that Mosi would take. Mosi stopped to help that man too.

Because of his sinister heart, but thinking that he is clever and not evil, Adama sees a bird in a thicket and throws a net over it on the path to the Sacred Forest. He knew that Mosi would stop to help that bird.

In that same village, there was a young mother who had to work to make ends meet. She was a market seller, and she would leave her child with the old woman to care for while she worked. Somehow

Adama knew all of that also and with the extra mile the old woman had to walk, she left the child unattended for longer than expected and the child became very hungry.

Adama had approached the young mother at the market and tried some of his smooth talking on her, but she wasn't interested. It did, however, delay her from returning home to get her child. She did not know that the old woman was gone for much longer than usual.

Adama didn't see any of this as sabotage; he saw it as strategy; he both wanted to get to the ancient wealth in the forest, and also to win the gold the king was offering back in the Kingdom of Uzuri. He thought it was either how you do business, or how you win a competition. He also thought the quickest one would win.

Adama gave no thought that he must hurry back for the sake of the Kingdom, he only thought of hurrying so he would win.

Mosi was in no way competing with Adama, except it would be nice to marry

Princess Neema. Adama was focused and determined to get to the Forest first, locate the wealth and claim it for himself and then return home to Uzuri as a hero and get all that gold that the king was offering to the winner of the contest. Oh, wouldn't his dad be surprised to see his son so rich, thought Adama.

Espionage and sabotage cost money. Just to find out these details took manpower, and Adama had hired and paid several men, whose hearts were also not pure, to find out how to interfere with Mosi's progress toward the Sacred Forest.

The Sacred Forest

Adama reached the forest first and bolted in like he owned it. He treated the forest like he treated people, as if he owned them. He crushed things under his feet; he broke limbs from their trees as if he had to thrash the forest to get to the wealth. Could he not realize that those branches were the children of those trees and were precious to them?

In all his ransacking, he didn't know where the ancient wealth was. It is not as though there was anyone to ask. Even if he saw someone, who is going to tell him where there is a stash of wealth?

Who would he ask? He never has time for people, he never stops to talk to them, except to trick them out of something, or take something from them, just because he wants it. Remember, Adama is looking for the wrong thing anyway.

Adama saw some beautiful fruit and began to pick it and eat, eat, eat. He didn't realize how hungry he was. He had never tasted fruit like this before and didn't really know what it was. He just knew it looked good and after eating it he felt kind of happy.

He wandered a while longer, but was unable to find the ancient wealth.

He became thirsty and frustrated, after chopping down so many trees, and destroying parts of the Sacred Forest.

Adama saw a stream and took a long drink from it, like he was a camel. He didn't realize how thirsty he was. The fruit or the water, or both of those things together made him delirious. He went into what he thought was a trance. Everything was spinning.

A large forest *spirit* appeared, but he thought he was dreaming.

The *spirits* were looking and had seen Adama creating all this destruction. They sent their messenger to let Adama know they were angered by his greed, and lack of respect for the Forest. They cursed him to wander endlessly. Even if Adama had been awake or fully aware to hear this, he wouldn't have believed it--, he thinks that nothing can happen to him. His rich dad always protected him and gave him everything he wanted. Everything.

While Adama slept off his fruit trance, Mosi arrived at the entrance of the forest. He spoke to the forest and told them his name and where he was from. He asked if he could go to the ancient well and carry some water to his people. There were just forest sounds. No one answered his salutation, but that is what he was told to do, so he did it. After Mosi spoke, it seemed that the birds got louder, happier and a gentle breeze blew with a sweet smell to it. When Mosi arrived, the forest seemed to welcome him.

When he entered the forest, he thought it was the prettiest thing he had ever seen. All the animals were different, they were more colorful, more beautiful, the greenery was greener, the flowers were bigger and brighter. The fruits were amazing, but they belonged to the trees, not to him. And because of the kind old woman who had fed him, he was not hungry.

So, Mosi kept walking ahead.

Mosi got lost on the path but at a banana tree there was a monkey that became his friend. The cutest little African monkey came up to him. When Mosi realized the monkey would follow him, he named the monkey, Kima. Kima began to swing from tree to tree to show Mosi the way to the ancient well which was hidden in a deeper part of the forest.

The trees parted, they seemed to bow, to reveal a glowing path. Mosi had another guide. It was the bird he had freed from the thicket earlier. One on each side, his new friends, Kima and the beautiful bird both indicated the way to the ancient well.

At the end of the path, he found it. It was the ancient well, the one the oracle, Madam Zubedi had spoken of. It shimmered with pure water.

Mosi filled his gourd and returned to the village. He never saw Adama who was asleep in some other part of the Forest the entire time that Mosi was retrieving the enchanted water.

Only Good Manners

As he left the Sacred Forest, Mosi was sure to say, "Thank You for letting me take this water back to my homeland. Thank you for letting me come into your beautiful forest." Mosi was sure to say, "Thank you," to God who made all these things, including the forest, and commenting on the glory of it all.

"Oh," he added, "and I had a banana. Thank you," he said as he walked peacefully out of the Sacred Forest.

These are the actions of a pure-hearted person.

A Hero's Welcome

Mosi went home the same way he came. The old woman had a delicious meal for him, as she had promised, and he really enjoyed it. The lady with the little girl gave him more water for his trip back to his own home.

Mosi entered the gates of the kingdom like a hero with the gourd of water in his lanky arms. There was hope for the kingdom now. Everyone was delighted.

He went to the palace with the water gourd and presented it to the King. He really used the gourd as an excuse to see Princess Neema and to show off just a little. She smiled; she was impressed.

Mosi, along with Madam Zubedi went out into the village square and poured the Living Water onto the ground to heal the ground from the Curse of the Half Curse, that was really a curse of half drought. The moment the water touched the parched soil, the land bloomed with life. It was vibrant and lush and beautiful just as the foliage and trees were in the Sacred Forest.

The Kingdom Rejoices

When Mosi returned with the water from the sacred forest the kingdom rejoiced.

The king kept his promise and offered Mosi great wealth and Princess Neema's hand in marriage. Mosi is now the new hero of the kingdom.

Mosi, however, humbly declined the wealth, but chose to marry Princess Neema not just for her beauty but for her kind heart.

It was a perfect day for a wedding, and the ceremony had already started, but suddenly Mosi's monkey came into the wedding chapel. Kima had followed him from the forest, and then to the delight of everyone, to Mosi's wedding. Everyone thought he was so cute.

Kima had with him another gourd of water. He had carried it all the way from the enchanted well in the Sacred Forest. Mosi remembers seeing that very same little gourd by the ancient well. Kima gave the little water gourd to Mosi. Even though Mosi had been told not to drink the water from the forest, he realized this was water from the well, not the stream. Kima waited until Mosi drank the water.

Suddenly Mosi turned ruggedly handsome. His nose straightened and his ears didn't seem so large anymore. The women swooned. Mosi didn't see what they saw because he had always avoided mirrors, so his new handsomeness never went to his head, and he never became a narcissist like Adama.

But Mosi did notice that he walked better than he used to. One leg was no longer crooked; it was no longer shorter than the other. How can a man without a crooked heart have a crooked leg? All things were made better than new for Mosi, the new kingdom hero.

The villagers, ashamed of how they had treated Mosi, came to respect and honor him, now, not for his good looks, but for his kind heart.

They asked him about Adama, but Mosi honestly could say that he had not seen him.

Stuck in the Forest

Adama, meanwhile, was lost in the forest. The sacred forest is very sensitive to the spirits and souls of those who enter it, and it does not like those with bad character traits. Adama was lost of his own making.

Wandering, as he did every day, one day Adama came to a clearing that looked rather familiar. He thought it was his former home in the kingdom of Uzuri, but it was not. Something was drawing him there; it was the village of the two beautiful women that he had assaulted. A mob came after him and he ran for his life, wishing that he had stayed lost.

As soon as he wished that, suddenly he was back in the Sacred Forest, eating that beautiful fruit and drinking from the stream that he should not drink from. His head began to do that *thing* again, like it was spinning. He just sat down and went through this trance or brain fog all over again. His life was wasting away. Why was he trapped here?

"Dad," he said aloud, "Dad, why don't you come rescue me?" Adama soon realized that he said that every day. It had become his prayer.

Adama often rehearsed his journey from Uzuri to the sacred Forest. Retracing his steps and most often with regret he recalled sabotaging Mosi. He thought he was the big man in that village where he assaulted not one but two women. By the time Adama got to the Sacred Forest, a place that only accepted those with pure hearts, his heart was filthy. It was absolutely filthy.

Neither then, nor now, Adama had no way of seeing that he was an evil person. As far as he was concerned, he was beautiful or at least handsome and he was rich. His father was important, so how could there be anything wrong with him? He had the perfect life. He justified in his own mind that there certainly was nothing wrong with him.

Years Ago

Years ago, the Sacred Forest wasn't sacred; it was the opposite of sacred. It was horrid and the place of horror. It was a place where the lusty and the greedy flocked to in order to become wealthy, rich, and powerful. Those were the types who would do anything for money, success, and wealth. Anything. But there still were rules that had to be followed in the Forest.

Years ago, when the Sacred Forest wasn't sacred, a young man named Madu traveled from Nigeria, across the Continent to Kenya. He did this to seek wealth and fortune. He did this to enter into the Forest of Fortune, that is what it was called then. There, this young man planned to get great wealth.

Madu was one of those people who went into the Forest for power, but he got kicked out of the Forest and was forbidden to ever again return.

Mzee Madu

Mzee Madu is what he is called now that he has wealth, power, and an air of sophistication. This is Adama's father.

Adama's very wealthy father was up in age and could not go on a quest to find his lost son. Well, that's what he would have people to believe.

Mzee Madu sits in a special chair that is a wheelchair, but no one knows--, no one but his personal assistant and driver, Mason. He has his trusted caregiver place him in that chair before meetings and he holds court. He even gets his assistant to cross his legs for him, he says it makes him look more natural. No one knows.

He goes nowhere and he has everyone to believe he is reclusive – he's proud and doesn't want anyone to see the wheelchair.

Under the cover of night, or very early in some mornings his caregiver/driver, Mason will take him out when he thinks no one will see him. Mzee Madu does not want to be considered weak. He has a lot of pride.

We know that people cannot or should not go into the enchanted Sacred Forest if they do not have a pure heart. Adama was fruit off the tree of his father's impure heart. In addition to the wheelchair, Madu's soiled heart is why Mzee Madu could not go into the forest to rescue his only son. And it is why Adama went into the forest so disrespectfully.

Because he couldn't go on this rescue mission, Mzee Madu sent two of his servants, but they stopped short of the Sacred Forest because of fear, and did not go in. They came back and reported that they did not see Adama anywhere.

They did not even look in the Forest for Adama. I told you the people of this kingdom have issues with having pure hearts. Mzee Madu fired both of them, even though they had been in his employ for years.

Next, Adama's rich father, Mzee Madu hired two men to go. They told Mzee Madu that they needed more money because of having to hire a search party. Mzee quadrupled the money and gave it to them, but those men did not go, they only stole the money and ran away to another kingdom.

More impure hearts. Not only that, the Forest was slowly in it's own way taking away the wealth that Madu got from the Forest all those years ago. In his emotional state, however, Madu was not able to see that. People were taking money for jobs and work that they were not doing and were never going to do. In Madu's eyes, if he were to see clearly, that would be stealing. But, how did he even get all this money in the first place?

By stealing from the Forest of Fortune.

Adama's father then tried to hire two more men to go look for Adama and saying he would pay them double what he paid the others, but they wouldn't get paid until they got back with his son, Adama.

Those men refused.

Everyone in that kingdom knew that if you did not have an absolutely pure heart, and you dared enter the Sacred Forest, you might not ever be seen again.

A few weeks later Adama's father tried again, but no one anywhere around would go look for Adama because none of them have a pure heart, and they know it.

Adama's father is a man of wealth, power and connections, but he is frustrated because he cannot now save what truly matters, his son, Adama. He's wealthy. He is powerful, but he can't save Adama.

Mzee Madu has always been a powerful man, but now is he losing that power?

The Estate

Mzee Madu's estate is nestled in western Kenya, near the Kakamega Forest, the last remnant of the once-great Guineo-Congolian rainforest.

His estate is a modern-meets-traditional compound: high walls, Maasai stonework, carved wooden doors from Lamu, ancestral masks from across the continent. He is either an East African man, loaded with West African gold, or a formerly West African man who migrated to East Africa and attained wealth from all over. But it is a lonely estate. Mzee Madu quickly fires anyone who doesn't do his bidding, so the place gets bigger and bigger as fewer and fewer people live there or work there. Some days you can almost hear an echo in the mansion.

Madu migrated to Kenya decades ago, as a younger man chasing wealth, power, and perhaps escaping whatever he did to whoever he did it to back home in Nigeria.

He built a vast empire of plantations and trade routes. He has connections to politicians, even spiritual leaders; Mzee Madu made sure he was connected to everyone of importance and power.

. To most, he is a *man of respect*, even awe. But the land knows what he did. The land not only remembers, but it will testify against you at any time, if you are not careful.

Mzee Madu cannot go to the Sacred Forest; he has been banned from it. *Why*? In his youth, Mzee Madu entered the Forest and disrespected it. He took something or some things from the Forest, and everyone knows you don't steal from the Sacred Forest or the Forest of Fortune, or whatever a forest is called.

When Madu first got to the forest, he wandered a bit, but from his bag he retrieved a piece of weathered leather. A map. He studied it, traced the lines with his index finger. After he got his bearings, he began to walk. He went straight toward the hidden groves. He was headed straight for the Grove of Wealth, the Grove of Power, the Grove of Fortune, and the Grove of Fate.

The Forest knew that no one knew how to go directly to those groves unless someone had told them. WizWali is who the Forest supposed sold secrets to this young man and sent him to the Forest. WizWali was always selling secrets, but he never came to the Forest himself, so they could never make him stop.

But even after he got there, the Forest surmised, this young upstart wouldn't know what to do, what to look for or how to acquire anything in those groves.

Or would he?

The Sacred Trees

Madu quickened his steps and arrived at the Three Groves, the fourth grove was a little distance away. These groves were no more or less beautiful than any of the other trees or groves in the Forest, unless you know what to look for.

Madu went directly to the Grove of Wealth and chose a certain tree within that grove, as if he knew, and laid down at it and went to sleep. He slept under that tree until morning and then arose as soon as the sun came up. He saw and captured the one golden leaf that the tree had given him for being there all night.

Next, he went to the Grove of Power and selected a certain tree and sat there until dark. Just before dark he offered the tree the golden leaf from the Tree of Wealth, and went to sleep under that tree. He didn't eat, he didn't drink anything, he didn't relieve himself at all. He just slept until dawn again.

In the morning, the Tree of Power had given him a golden twig. He found it when he woke up.

Next, he went to the Grove of Fortune, offered it the golden twig and went to sleep under that tree. This was the third night that he did the very same thing. At dawn the next morning, he had planned to leave the Forest. But---, the Tree of Fortune hadn't given him anything, however. Nothing. Nothing at all.

This angered him tremendously.

Many who came through the Forest had paid WizWali a lot of money – everything they had, for the map and the information on how to manipulate the Forest and the trees and the groves to get everything that they wanted.

Madu stood screaming at the tree, demanding a gift from the tree to indicate that fortune would be his for the rest of his life, but the tree stood there, offering him nothing.

In a rage, Mzee began to shake the branches of the Tree of Fortune. He bruised the branch and damaged the leaves, and he even started kicking the tree and damaged the bark on the tree's trunk.

It was at this point the Mzee jumped up, swung from a low branch and it snapped, he took the entire branch, even though it was small – he was determined that he wasn't leaving with nothing.

You know what, thought Madu, I'm taking everything. I've been in this forest for three nights, no food, no water – nothing. I'm not leaving with nothing. No, I'm leaving with everything.

Madu took back the golden twig from the Tree of Fortune that he had offered just last night, and then he ran to the Tree of Power and took back the golden leaf, then as fast as his 24-year-old legs could carry him, he raced forward to a fourth tree--, the Tree of Fate. Madu defaced and defiled the tree by relieving himself on it. After that he ran for the exit of this forest. He was determined not to leave empty handed.

As he ran, the Forest *spirits* tried to restrain him, but he broke free. He ran a few more steps, but then a strong wind came against his body to push him back. He strained but kept pushing forward.

Considering himself more clever than anyone, Madu squat to the ground and rolled himself into a ball and simply rolled out of the Forest. How could that happen? It's an enchanted forest, that's how. All kinds of things can happen in there.

Madu had to know that anything you give the forest, you cannot take it back. You also cannot harm any of the trees in the forest. You do not deface the forest, nor do you relieve yourself against a sacred tree. If the forest does not give you whatever you came for, you cannot force it.

In addition, Madu had broken the law of the third night. WizWali either didn't know, or hadn't told Madu about the third night. Wiz Wali was all about getting paid, not following rules. The Tree of Fortune required the golden twig **and** Madu's clothes, but he kept them on, this is why the tree gave him nothing.

Would he have done it if he had known? Would he have slept in his birthday suit?

We don't know, do we?

Young Madu was the worst. He was worse than WizWali who the Forest blamed for sending this one to ruin its groves. Madu hadn't even met WizWali, didn't know him and never paid him a cent.

Madu had stolen the map from a drunk man who talked too much, in a bar. This is why Madu didn't know all the rules of the Forest of Fortune. All he knew is he wanted to go there, and he wanted what the Forest would offer.

Madu rolled out of the Forest safely and then stood to his feet, exuberant.

The Forest *spirits* let him live, but only if he never again sought the *deep places*, because if he did, they would restrain him, detain him, and the trees would lock him in forever because he owed the Forest. He owed the offerings, he owed for the damage, and he owed for taking that branch and the golden leaf and the golden twig.

The Sacred Forest *knows* Madu. The forest doesn't forget. If it did, the other forests that communicate with it will remind it of those who have offended the Forest, or any forest for that matter.

The land remembers.

The Forest senses his stolen spiritual legacy. Madu, the Forest thundered, "You have a limited time to return to the Forest what belongs to the Forest."

Mzee raised his fist in defiance with his back to the Forest and laughed as *he* showed the forest his back.

Right then, the Forest *spirits* let him know, "Madu if you enter this Forest, or any forest again, the trees will close behind you. Forever."

The Forest Took It

At age 24, young Madu was pretty impressed with himself. He had gotten the map for free, he had made his way across the Continent, found the Forest of Fortune, and had gotten wealth and power. After leaving the Forest, Madu was very proud of himself. *Some years went by, Mzee Madu was sure that he had won. He began to* get a lot of wealth. Things started working out for him in business. He seemed to have favor with people.

He didn't have good fortune though. Sometimes he had misfortunes.

His first wife couldn't conceive. That is the first thing the Forest took. Madu raged at her night and day until she couldn't take it anymore. One day while he was out at work, she packed up her things and just left. She went back to her family.

His second wife, Adama's mother did conceive but she left Mzee because he was overbearing. That is the next thing the Forest took. She also just packed up her things. She had stood at the front door before leaving, she hesitated as to whether she should take Adama but decided not to since that would mean that Madu would follow her as long as she had his child with her. With tears in her eyes, for Adama, not for Madu, she turned her back and left the toddler, only two years old standing there, himself also crying.

Madu was at work and she new the baby nurse would come running to Adama as soon as she heard him cry. She left quickly because she didn't want anyone on the estate to see her leave. She didn't want there to be any clue as to what direction she took when she left.

Mzee tried to get another wife, but his ways were so abrasive that no woman wanted to be with him. Whether he showed his money or not, they didn't want him. When he was young, even when he was older --, the ladies kept turning him down. He was most often lonely, but when he got into a relationship, he was not a nice man, it is as though his ugly ways drove women away. That is the third thing the Forest took.

Growing up in a big mansion without a woman's touch and no loving environment, Adama became an ungrateful, bitter son who barely spoke to his father. The fourth thing.

It was ten years later. One night, Mzee had a dream where the Forest *spirits* spoke to him saying, "Old man, you want to roll out of the Forest with what belongs to us? Then roll you shall." That was the fifth thing the Forest took. Mzee Madu never put it together that it was the powers in the Forest robbing him of good fortune and a happy life, even though he had money and power.

More misfortune hit Madu. One day while unloading a merchant ship he had an accident that affected his spine and that is what put him in the wheelchair.

And now, the worst misfortune of all: His only child, Adama is lost in the forest. It has been four years and Madu doesn't know how much more he can take.

If he had known that Adama was planning to go to the Forest, he would have stopped him.

If only Mzee Madu hadn't been so full of pride and had spent more time with his child, he would have told his son about the Forest of Fortune, but he kept it a secret. And, as a secret, it had become a weapon against his son, his heir, his legacy.

No, Old Man

After Mosi had returned to Uzuri with a hero's welcome, Mzee Madu was very troubled: where is his son, Adama? He *tried* once, secretly, to go after Adama. His driver took him there and they arrived early one morning. Madu even wheeled himself to the edge of the Forest. But the Forest wouldn't let him in.

The Forest *spirits* said, "Enter at your own risk because you will not be coming out, Old Man."

Thick vines, like snakes, coiled around the wheels of his ornate chair. If you stared at these vines, you did not see them move, but as soon as you looked away, suddenly they had crept over to Madu's wheelchair and then intertwined themselves through those golden wheelchair spokes of the wheels. The Forest spoke: No, Old Man. *"You, who have lived a thousand lives but never paid the price —, turn back."*

Mzee Madu turns and speaks to his driver Mason: Mason why don't you go in and look for Adama? Mason's eyes got very big, and he shook his head aggressively. Sir, if I don't come out, how will you get back home? No one knows we are here, and the people around here don't know how to drive cars, many of them have never seen a car.

Oh, Mason, you're right, what was I thinking?

The Forest knows Adama – they know him by his blood—, it's the blood of Mzee Madu. They want Adama to pay for his father's debts.

Mzee Madu is barred in more ways than one. He is barred by the forest *spirits*, by the land, by the impurity of his own heart. People may not know that forests speak to one another in their roots and by the winds.

This forest, which once was called the Forest of Fortune, was defiled so many times by so many evil, greedy, desperate people that it put up its barriers and blocked everyone who does not have a pure heart. It is now considered to be a sacred forest.

Another night, weeks after Adama vanished, Madu wheeled himself to the forest's edge. The air grew heavy. The forest *spirits* said, "The sins of the father."

Then the trees began to creak, bending toward him. His wheels stuck in the earth. He found he could go backward, but not forward. So backward he went and got Mason to put him back in his limousine and drive him back to Uzuri.

Madu's legacy is at risk because if he dies without an heir, his enemies take everything. Adama is the heir; the Forest has his only heir. Is the Forest still taking from Madu for taking from it all those years ago?

Mzee Madu is caught in a spiritual checkmate; if he moves toward the Forest, he loses. But if he stays, he may lose *everything anyway*.

He desperately yells, "Adama, Adama, are you in there? Where are you, son?" Madu realized that he said to himself or out loud, "Where are you son?" every day. It had become his prayer.

Inside the Forest, Adama was delirious on the magical fruit that he should not be eating, and the water that he should not be drinking. He was tripping as usual. Adama never did learn not to eat that fruit or drink that water.

In the middle of his latest head trip, Adama thought he heard his name being called. He thought he heard his father's voice, but after all this time, why should he believe that?

Mason had gotten tired of bringing the grieving Mzee Madu to the Forest's edge, it was every week, and it was now four years. The old man had aged a thousand years. His legs were no stronger and he cried himself to sleep almost every night.

He could find no one to go look for Adama--, but then it hit him—

MOSI.

Purehearted Mosi

He would ask Mosi. He would tell Mosi. He would pay Mosi, he would bribe Mosi, he would even beg Mosi. Whatever it took, that's what he would do. Mzee Madu was desperate. He had come to know that Mosi was about the only man in the kingdom with a pure heart.

Why didn't he think of this before? Between you and me, Mzee didn't think of asking Mosi before because Adama had competed against Mosi to get the sacred water years ago, and Mzee considered Mosi an enemy because his precious spoiled son, Adama didn't win.

Mosi, however, never considered Adama nor his father an enemy. That is one of the differences in a pure hearted person and one with an impure heart.

"Mason, drive me to Mosi's house."

"Mosi's house? Mosi married the princess but he didn't move into the palace?"

"Nope." Mosi was still on his land and farming it and Princess Neema was by his side. Their love had blossomed.

They now had two little kids. Mzee fought back tears, he had no child now, no grandchild. "Adama, Adama," he lamented in the back seat of his limousine. "Where are you son?"

As they approached Mosi's farm, Mzee pulled himself together.

"Mason, after you park, ask Mosi to come over to the car and speak with me."

"Yes sir."

While he waited in the car, Mzee looked out over Mosi's farm, it was lush and green and healthy. All this, he thought must have been because he brought back that special water all those years ago. What Mzee didn't know is during the year of the half drought, Mosi's farm was never hurt by the brown blight. The curse would never have alighted on Mosi or his land. Mosi didn't know that his farm would be spared, but even if he did, he still would have gone to help others. Mosi, with his pure heart had a right relationship with the land so his farm and his crops were never affected. Still, Mosi went to the Sacred Forest to get the sacred water to help the others of the kingdom.

Once Mosi was in the back seat beside him, Mzee Madu confessed with distress in his voice, "Mosi, thank you for coming to speak with me. It's Adama, we need to find Adama. I believe he is still in the Forest."

Mosi was shocked, "Adama is still in the Forest? Sir, how can that be? I am sorry, I did not know. There have been so many rumors. People said that he went abroad to study."

"Mosi, would you be willing to go back to the Forest and search for Adama, for me, for this old man?" Then his voice changed to almost pleading, "I'll do anything you ask, I'll give you any amount for your troubles."

"Sir, I have children now, so I know how it would feel if my son were lost. I will go and look for Adama. There is no charge, Sir. There is no fee. No one knew but Mosi's farm was very profitable. Everything he touched prospered; he had more money than he needed, more than his family would ever need. But he wasn't showy and didn't wear it in outfits or hold fancy parties, or brag.

It wasn't about Mosi not taking money, it was that he would go to look for Adama. Mzee couldn't help himself, he broke down and he grabbed Mosi's arm and said, "Thank you, thank you, thank you.

"You don't have to walk, Mosi. We can drive you there. Do you need anyone to go with you?"

"No sir, not in particular. I am friends with the Forest; we know one another.

Mzee hung his head, yeah, the Forest knows him too, they are just not friends.

Too often men with impure hearts choose to make friends with silver and gold, instead of making friends with the land that provides the money and wealth--, the silver and the gold.

Or better, still, make friends of the God over the land.

He Made a Choice

The curse the Forest *spirits* put on Adama, that he would roam endlessly but still remain lost, no one was able to break the curse, because no one knew about it. Not even Adama knew because he kept eating that fruit and drinking the water and not realizing that he was cursed by the forest *spirits*, even though they told him. It was as though his understanding or memory was broken.

To add to that, Adama when he had wandered into the village of the two ladies that he hurt and was fleeing for his life had wished to stay lost, so he had **agreed** with the curse, making it double hard to break.

Adama stayed lost for years, and by legend, became known as the Lost Man of the Forest. Women and mothers warned their friends and daughters against going near that forest because that Lost Man of the Forest was ruthless and would attack them and take their virtues.

Another reason Adama stayed in the forest was to look for the *ancient wealth*. He was determined to find it. Although his mind was altered by the food and water there, he never forgot about hidden wealth that he lusted for. Yet, he never did find that wealth.

All those years Adama was in the Forest, he never noticed the beauty of the Forest nor the value of the land. A person may not see value in another, unless it is value that they want to take from that person. A person may not see the beauty of nature or the value of a forest or a land, unless they first see wealth, riches, or other things of value that they can take.

The Sacred Forest was beautiful to Mosi. It was dark and sinister to Adama. The heart sees what it, itself is: Mosi saw a pretty forest. Adama saw dark land that should be destroyed. Mosi saw a kindhearted woman when he looked at Princess Neema because he, himself was kindhearted. Adama looked in the same direction as Mosi at the same time, yet Adama only saw gold. Wealth was the whole desire of his heart.

When a man prefers the byproduct to the real thing, that man may be looking for shortcuts or glory. When people don't see you as you really are it could be because they are looking through a heart that is not pure.

Mosi Returns to the Forest

On the day of the Rescue-Adama Mission, from the back of the limo, Mosi directs Mason on where the entrance of the Forest is.

"The entrance?" questioned Mzee. "There's an entrance?"

"Yes Sir, a dedicated place where you enter the Forest. Like a door to a person's house, you come in through the entrance. We must enter the Forest at the entrance, and with respect. It is alive, Sir."

Mzee mutters under his breath, "That's for sure." Mason takes Mzee out of the car and puts him in his ornate wheelchair. Mzee is expecting Mosi to stare at him, but Mosi does not. It's as though he's never even around any purehearted people before. It is confusing to him, but at that moment his pride is beginning to drop, it is beginning to fade.

Mosi gets to the entrance of the Forest and stops. He greets the forest.

Mzee cannot roll any closer, but he is bewildered by Mosi speaking to the Forest.

"*What*?" he whispers under his breath.

Kima hears Mosi's voice and swings wildly to meet him. He jumps on Mosi's shoulder as if to say, *Hey Man, how you doing? Where have you been*? There is a little lady monkey with Kima – looks like he got married too. The two monkeys bounced happily onto a tree branch and then into the Forest.

Mosi saw the beautiful bird that he had rescued, but now there are two of them. Everyone has paired up and things are blossoming in the forest. It is beautiful.

"Hi, my name is Mosi, I was here several years ago to get some water from the sacred well. Thank you very much; that worked out perfectly for our kingdom. I'm here to rescue my friend, Adama. Is he here?"

Adama heard his name. He really heard it.

He ran toward the sound of his name ---, if that was still his name, no one had called it in so long! And he was beginning to get forgetful. He was wobbly but he walked toward the entrance of the Forest where he had heard his name called.

"Adama, his dad called out! Adama!"

Adama couldn't hear his dad, but he heard Mosi calling to him. There was purity and clarity and love in Mosi's voice, and Adama could hear it. He made his way to the entrance. He saw Mosi, but looked past him immediately and saw his dad!

"DAD! DAD!" he yelled loudly.

Mzee tried to roll his chair toward the boy, but the vines had looped around the wheelchair wheels, and he couldn't move.

Adama looked a little thin, but he looked as if he had aged 10 years in the past four. He tried to run toward his dad, but couldn't go past the entrance of the forest as if there was a force field between him and his father. He couldn't leave the Forest? Is this true? He couldn't leave?

"Dad, I can't get to you! Dad? Dad! Get me out of here!"

Amid sobs, Mzee Madu said, "Son, you're alive, you're okay. We came to get you, Adama."

"Well, dad, I need a good bath and some sleep and a haircut, and…"

"Yes, Adama, but you're okay?"

"Mosi? Mosi? Is that you? asked Adama. Do you look different? Mosi, you came for me? For *me*?" Adama rattled off so many questions without a pause in between. It seemed like ages since he talked to another human.

"Yes, Adama, I didn't know you were still here. I don't know if I look different, I don't look in mirrors.

Adama, we all thought you'd come back and traveled abroad for studies. Yes, I came here for you," replied Mosi, all in one breath trying to answer every question.

"No man, I've been stuck here. Like forever. How long have I been here?"

No one answered that question, but they had other questions for the Forest captive: "Why, Adama? Why have you been stuck here? What happened?"

"I don't know."

To ease his mind, Mzee asked, "Son, didn't you want to come home?"

Adama hesitated a moment and said, "Yes Dad, but I was still looking for the ancient wealth."

Mosi heard that and realized that it didn't make any sense. So, he again spoke to the Forest to try to get Adama out of captivity, "I--, I--, I'm here for Adama, did he do anything to offend the Forest?"

The Forest answered, "Yes."

Mosi glared at Adama.

"What did he do?" Mosi asked as if he was Adama's father, even with his own father, Mzee Madu sitting right there, as if he didn't know that a father corrects and teaches his son, if he really loves him. All Mzee Madu had ever done was to spoil that boy.

"Destruction" answered the Forest. He came in here like a madman and chopped down trees and destroyed things. He ate our fruit and drank from the stream without permission."

"Adama, you didn't?" accused Mosi.

"I did." he confessed quickly.

"Did you apologize?"

"I didn't know that I had to apologize."

"Apologize, Man."

"I'm sorry?"

"That was weak, Bruh. Apologize for real."

Spoiled brat Adama never had to apologize a day in is life. "I'm sorry. I'm sorry I chopped down trees. I'm sorry I ate your fruit and drank from the stream without permission." Adama spoke like a robot, just to get this over with as if he didn't even mean it.

Adama stopped and waited for the sighing rush of an answer through the trees. But, the Forest didn't answer.

Mosi elbowed Adama, urging him to say more, to apologize better. "I'm really sorry. Will you please forgive me?" Adama asked the Forest with real sincerity now.

Finally, "YES," answered the Forest *spirits.*

Mzee watched intently and was amazed at what was happening. He then spoke up and said, "Forest: I am Mzee Madu."

"We know who you are, Old Man."

"Yeah, I'm old now, but when I was my own son's age, I offended you too. I would like to apologize.

The Forest was quiet, very still and quiet.

"I am sorry, Mzee Madu continued, "will you also forgive *me*?" he asked, not knowing if what he had done to the Forest was even forgivable.

The silence seemed to last forever. Then the forest *spirits* said, "It took you long enough, Old Man."

Mzee sat in his ornate wheelchair and wept. Thinking to himself, "Is that all it took all this time? Manners? An apology?" It is at that point that Mzee Madu realized that pride is not his friend and has never been his friend. The weight of 25 years was lifted off Mzee at that exact moment. He had made peace with the land by simply apologizing for abusing it.

Monkey Business

Kima and his wife, Lady Kima came back to the men at the edge of the forest. Kima had a small gourd; it was filled with water from the sacred well. He handed it to Mzee Madu and indicated that he must drink it. The old man drank the water. His legs began to shake, to move. His spine quickened, he sat upright very strongly. He tried to stand; he could now stand. He could stand!

"DAD!" screamed Adama in shock and amazement. He hadn't seen his dad stand since Adama was 10 years old! "This is a miracle! This is a miracle, **DAD!**"

Lady Kima also had a water gourd and gave a drink to Adama. He drank the water. This was different water than water from the stream, it was sweeter, purer, very refreshing. Years of aging fell off Adama and he became handsome again, still disheveled, but handsome. A new energy was released within him so Adama dared take a step toward the edge of the forest.

Mzee Madu took his first step with the help of Mason toward his son. Then Mason let go. The force field was broken and Mzee Madu and Adama found each other and embraced for the first time in many, many years. Tears were flowing everywhere.

"Son."

"Dad, Father."

They wept some more and then both turned to Mosi pouring out thank you's. "Thank you, Mosi. Thank you."

Mosi, without being too pushy, says, "Thank God, not me. Now, turn to the forest and say Thank you, and let it know that you are leaving now." Father and son both did as they were told. That is real deliverance from pride for both of them to do something that someone else tells them to do instead of always issuing the commands.

Before turning to walk back to the car, Mzee Madu made a beautiful gesture, when he said to the Forest, I give you this gold chair. It is made of pure gold, and I hope you will take it in payment for the golden leaf and the golden twig and for the offenses that I made against the Forest, as well as for the damages that Adama caused to your arbors."

It was now the turn of the Forest to say, "Thank you." Finally, Mzee Madu and his son, Adama were released from the grip of the Forest. They had finally made amends and also made friends with it.

"Mosi, Mzee asked, How did you learn to talk to the Forest?"

"Oh, when I was on my way here the first time, I met several people who each told me things I needed to do to get into the Forest and get the water from the ancient well."

"Wizards?" asked Mzee, who was too well versed in this sort of thing.

"No, regular people. An old lady I helped carry firewood. A younger woman who was a seller in the village whose daughter I shared my lunch with. And you met Kima and the beautiful birds. We all made friends on the way here many years ago.

"As a matter of fact, I'd love to stop by and see them all and see how they are doing. And there was an old man, I'd like to look in on him, too. He's the one who told me never to relieve myself against a sacred tree."

"What!" Mzee Madu's head snapped toward Mosi, and he repeated in his mind, "Never relieve yourself against a sacred tree." So that's what he had done that offended the Forest so much? Well, yes--, among other things. That could be why he had been in that wheelchair for 20 years! Tears again began to stream from Mzee's eyes, burning his cheeks.

In the back of the limo on the way back to Uzuri, Adama and Mosi's conversation continued regarding visiting friends and former acquaintances. This was strange talk to Adama, going back where you came from?

Adama had burned so many bridges and had ruined so many relationships. Fruit doesn't fall far from the tree, *eh*?

Wait! It just hit him—, "Mosi, you got water from the ancient well?"

Yes, Adama, it's the water we came to the Forest to get in the first place. You know, to heal the drought of the kingdom. It's the same water that you and your dad drank already. I drank it too, some years ago, that is why I walk so much better than I used to.

"Oh--," said Adama, "it's an ancient well, not wealth?" Nobody knew what he was talking about, but Adama was glad he could hear clearly now. He realized that everything is not about money, gold and wealth. He chuckled to himself.

"Mosi, would it be okay if we drove you back to see your friends another day? I'd like to get Adama home and get him cleaned up and rested up first."

"Yes sir, that would be best. Another day will be fine. Thank you."

Lessons

Sometimes you can't properly leave a thing or a person until you make peace with it or them.

Always leave things and people better than you found them.

Always be on your best manners.

Be the best you can be always, and always expect the best from others.

That day both Adama and his father, Mzee Madu found the true wealth.

Don't let ugly ways erase the steps of where you came from, because if you visit again, your friends will be glad to see you.

A wellspring of life and love and healing is wealth.

Everyone is not your enemy.

The person you think is your enemy may end up being the best friend you ever had.

One Sunny Day

One fine day, early in the morning, Mzee Madu and his son Adama, chauffeur driven by Mason arrived at Mosi's farm. Adama jumped out looking fine and healthy and like himself again. He greeted Mosi and said, "If you like, my father says we can drive you back to the village near the Sacred Forest to visit your friends."

"Now?"

"Sure, now, if you like. And bring your family, we will make a day of it." Princess Neema and the kids were so excited to have an outing and meet some of the people that Mosi had met even years ago. Mosi had spoken of them more than once over the years.

Close to the village where they were going they saw the old man who had begged for help. Mosi had Mason to stop and he got out to greet him. Mosi said, "Come and meet my family and my friends."

The man came to the back window and spoke to everyone inside. Then he said, "I've never seen a car before."

Mzee Madu said, "We've got room, enter the car and we can give you a ride." The man smiled broadly and entered the car. It was only a short distance from where they picked him up to the village, but the ride in a car meant the world to him, it was quite an experience.

They drove up to the village in a limousine, in fine style. People came out from their village homes to see the spectacle. Mason slowed down to a snail's pace to be careful around the people who had never seen a car, much less a limousine. Mason brought the vehicle to a stop and all the people got out.

The widow woman that Mosi had helped that day years ago came to greet him. She tilted her head because he looked different, but when she looked in his eyes, she knew it was him. Mosi proudly introduced his wife, Princess Neema and their two children to the widow woman. Then Mosi decided to introduce the elderly man to the widow woman. The older gentleman said, "I've seen you walking to get firewood before, I'd be glad to help you if you like."

The widow woman blushed and said, "Thank you, that would be nice."

This widow woman loved to feed people. She said, "If you would do that, I can share a meal with you on firewood days. The man said, I'd like that, thank you."

From then on, the elderly man brought the widowed woman a little firewood each day, so she'd need him to bring her firewood the next day and then the next. They'd sit and dine together every day, keeping each other company. The man who sold firewood hired the old man to sell firewood while he was out chopping it. The elderly man also delivered wood to those who couldn't come to pick it up for themselves. By doing so, now he had a job and eating regularly he began to get healthier, stronger and grew some muscles.

The little girl that Mosi shared his lunch with was now 7 years old. She became like an instant big sister to Mosi's daughter, and they became best friends. The little girl's mother caught Mason's eye, and they just stood and smiled at one another. It was sweet, really. She didn't remember Adama, and he didn't remember her either, although he had flirted with her in the market on his way to the Forest four years ago.

Mzee Madu and Adama's hearts were warmed. Adama felt a little ashamed that he had sabotaged Mosi on the journey for the sacred water and had also interfered in the lives of these good people. He was embarrassed, really.

The feeling of family was foreign to Mzee Madu and Adama, but they instantly were delighted to be around all these joyful people of all ages. Mzee Madu was just so glad to be standing and able to walk around the village. Princess Neema and everyone was so appreciative to see how loved Mosi was.

Mzee Madu made up his mind right then and there; he wanted a family. It was time for Adama to have children so there would be life in that big, beautiful mansion again. Adama needed more than one child so his grandchild would not be an only and lonely again, repeating Adama's childhood.

Once back in the car, Mzee expressed himself to Adama, saying he would like to see Adama get married and start a family.

Adama hung his head and silent tears painted his face. He asked Mason to stop the car, and he did. He got out of the car and went around to the driver's door. Mason got out of the car and Adama spoke discreetly to him.

Adama got back into the limo and the car pulled off. This time they stopped in another village. Adama was going to face his past as well. He didn't leave that village in good standing, but he decided that if after twenty some years his father had apologized to the Sacred Forest, he should not leave things hanging. Adama decided that he would go back to the village where he had assaulted those two women and apologize. Adama felt that if he did this, he could move forward with his life. He also had planned, if necessary to compensate the women for their pain and hardships that he probably caused them.

They pulled up to the next small village. Everyone sat in the car for a while. There were onlookers but no one came to greet this long beast of a machine or the people in it.

Mzee said to Adama, "Son, why are we here?"

"Dad, I'm a changed man; I have to apologize to someone--, well to some people, actually."

Adama slowly got out. Part of him hoped that he wouldn't be recognized, because this place formed mobs quickly and he didn't want them to come after him again. But then he wanted to be recognized so he could ask of the two ladies that he offended years ago. Lamina, he remembered her name, and her friend, Kwamboka.

He saw a pretty middle-aged woman walking hand in hand with two little ones, a boy and a girl about the same age. Were they twins? Possibly. Adama gathered the nerve to ask, "Ma, excuse me, I'm looking for an old friend, Lamina. Do you know her?"

"Yes, I do; I know Lamina. What do you want with her?"

"I'm an old friend, I'd like to greet her, Ma."

"Follow me, I'm on the way to where she lives now."

By this time Mzee Madu and everyone else had gotten out of the car. The kids saw some other kids and they became fast friends and started playing together, as kids are known to do. They all walked a short distance to a small house that Adama did not remember. When Lamina heard the gathering and chattering of people outside her house, she came outside. She was stopped in her tracks when she saw Adama. She didn't know whether to be angered or happy but before she could express any emotion, Adama blurted out, "Lamina! It's Adama, I came to apologize to you. And if you will have me," Adama dropped on one knee and proposed marriage to her.

She burst out crying.

Mzee Madu had followed Adama and had caught up with him only when he had fallen to one knee. Madu exclaimed, "Adama! What are you doing? Who is this young lady?"

"Dad, years ago, I made this woman my wife and now I want to do everything respectfully and in order."

Mzee had a flashback of all the women he had proposed to who had turned him down, years ago after his second wife had left him. He desperately hoped this woman would accept so Adama would not experience the heartbreaks that he had felt over and again. Adama had already been through so much, his dad thought silently.

Amid sobs, Lamina accepted.

Everyone who was not already there, had caught up with the two and at Lamina's acceptance, they all smiled and applauded.

Relieved, Mzee Madu said, "Adama, please make introductions."

He started, but out of respect, Lamina first introduced the woman with the two little kids. This is Miss Ebele, she is Kwamboka's' mother and Mzee saw her beauty immediately and let her know right away that he liked her. She blushed. He said I would like to get to know you better, would you take a stroll with me, that is if you're not married and someone can watch your children.

"These are not my children, and I'm not married," she said.

As Mzee and the woman walked away, Lamina turned to Adama and said, "This is Ayo; he is mine and this is Nia; she is Kwamboka's."

"Kwamboka? Where is she?" Adama had planned to propose to her as well, as a second wife, but Lamina held his heart. Kwamboka got a scholarship and went to the UK to study. She became a doctor and is now working with Doctors Without Borders and has dedicated herself to helping people. She also met another doctor and they are happily married. Her mother, who went for a walk with your father, is raising her daughter--, your daughter.

"That's Kwamboka's mother?" I didn't know.

"Yes, Adama. You should have taken more time to get to know me--, us."

Lamina continued, "She and my son play together all the time; they are like --, well they <u>are</u> brother and sister."

"How is that? How do they have the same father?"

There was silence in the gathering, then Adama put it together better than he realized that he should not have eaten the Sacred Forest fruit or drank from the stream.

"*I* --, I, have children?" asked Adama in unbelief?

"Yes, you do," replied Lamina. "**We** do," she corrected herself.

"I'm so sorry, I did not mean to do that to you or Kwamboka, I'm sorry." Then he mumbled, "I should have kept all that ugly to myself."

Adama was so conflicted. He was sorry, but he was happy to see Lamina and that she would accept him as her husband and he was very happy that he had two beautiful children.

He wept, because he knew he was not deserving of such good fortune.

Adama stared at the two children and then gathered them both into his arms like a proud dad. They looked just like him; there was no question. He wondered why he never saw them. He had wandered to this village more than once in his four years of trying to wander out of the Sacred Forest. Perhaps that is what was drawing him back to this village.

Then he realized that he was chased from this village every time he wandered here, so how could he possibly see Lamina or Kwamboka, or these two beautiful children?

"Marry me, Lamina and we will have more, as many as you want." He asked her again, just to be sure.

Whether she accepted because she wanted to and had been secretly waiting for his return or whether she was tired of being alone since the other men now shunned her, we may not know. Whether she loved him or whether she wanted payback, we do not know. Perhaps she just wanted her child, and the child of her friend, Kwamboka to have a father. Only time will tell that. But this meant taking the little girl from Kwamboka's mother. Lamina didn't think this would be possible or if it was, it would not go over well. Kwamboka's mother had no other family.

But still there was joy for Lamina as she was going to be getting married, finally.

To add to that joy, when Mzee Madu got back he had proposed to Kwamboka's mother and she had accepted. In African culture, marriages are often arranged, but many times it is instant that a man knows he has met his wife, and he proposes right away.

The Fortunate

In a few short months the Madu compound was full of life. Mzee Madu had his own wife. Adama was married with a beautiful wife and two kids. Mosi, Princess Neema and their two kids came almost every Sunday for dinner and the children played gleefully on the lawn.

Once a month Mason went to the village to see the market vendor with the little daughter. Once a month he picked up the young lady with the little daughter from the village and they'd all spend the day together. The two became a couple. Within a few months he had convinced Mzee Madu to let her come to the compound as a cook and they married and became a little family themselves.

Mzee Madu's compound finally was fulfilling its potential as a grand, palatial, joyful loving home. Good Fortune was finally smiling on him, and everyone was the happiest they had ever been.

The End

More Lessons

In the end, Uzuri learned a valuable lesson: true beauty lies in one's actions, not in good looks.

Adama could neither complete nor return from a sacred mission because his heart was not pure.

When you are looking for the wrong thing, most likely you will never find it. Sometimes when you are looking for the wrong thing you should pray to never find it.

If you're going to pray, pray to the right father.

If you're looking for the Son, look for the right Son.

As the saying in the kingdom of Uzuri goes, "A kind heart shines brighter than the finest gold."

The tale of Mosi and Adama became a cherished story passed down through generations, reminding all who heard it of the power of humility, kindness, and inner beauty.

After Adama's ugly actions in the village against those two young women, the people all began to see him as ugly.

Mosi never looked in a mirror to see how handsome he had become on the outside, while his inside was still beautiful. Still, once an ugly person gets with a beautiful person, you will never again convince him that they were ever ugly.

Inner ugly shows up on the outside.

Inner beauty will always show up on the outside.

So, keep your ugly to yourself, and don't give your pretty away.

Never wish to remain lost.

& never agree with a curse.

For more tales of power, betrayal, and redemption read other books by Nia Zola and also tune in to her channel on You Tube, Africa Untold Tales.

Books by Nia Zola

The Prince Has a Big Snake, https://a.co/d/bpzUH2M

You may view the abbreviated You Tube video version of this story on the Africa Untold Tales channel. It is entitled: ***JANGO: The Scent of Trouble.*** https://www.youtube.com/watch?v=NMRl qv18_uM

Book: **The Bewitching of Jango**, https://a.co/d/b8m7EVz

There are other fine stories on that channel as well.
https://www.youtube.com/@AfricaUntold-llc

www.ingramcontent.com/pod-product-compliance
Lightning Source LLC
Chambersburg PA
CBHW051259170626
46809CB00004B/1728